JAMES STEVENSON

The Great Big Especially Beautiful Easter Egg

MULBERRY BOOKS
New York

pocket next page

Library of Congress Cataloging in Publication Data
Stevenson, James (date)
The great big especially beautiful Easter egg.
Summary: At Easter, a man tells his two grandchildren
how he searched many years ago for a special Easter
egg to give to his friend Charlotte.
[1. Easter eggs—Fiction.   2. Easter—Fiction]
I. Title.   PZ7.S84748Gr 1983   [E]   82-11731
ISBN 0-688-09355-8

"Guess what day this is, Grandpa!" said Louie.
"I haven't the foggiest," said Grandpa.

"Easter!" said Mary Ann.
"Really?" said Grandpa.
"We're going to hunt for eggs!"
 said Louie.
"Did you ever hunt for eggs,
 Grandpa?" asked Mary Ann.
"Why, yes, I did," said Grandpa.
"But it was a long time ago.
 I was about your age...."

I was very fond of the girl
next door. Her name was Charlotte.

Every Easter I picked violets,
and gave them to Charlotte.

But one year, the night before Easter...

The next morning, I got up
very early and waited.
At last, I saw something coming....

Suddenly,
I remembered
something.

There was a wishbone that had never been used!

We landed in the snow.

We tiptoed along until

we came to a big nest. Strange bird calls were coming from it."

SURE! JUST COME CRASHING THROUGH THE SNOW SCREAMING 'HELLO'-- SURE! SURE!

I'LL BE EXTRA CAREFUL BECAUSE I WANT TO GIVE IT TO A FRIEND OF MINE!
VERY WELL.. HOW ABOUT THIS ONE?
PERFECT! SHE'LL LOVE IT!
E-EASY DOES IT.. GENTLY.. GENTLY...
THAT'S RIGHT.. TIPTOE!

"Did you fly back home
on the wishbone wish?"
asked Louie.
"No indeed—that wish
was only one-way, not
a round trip!
We had to climb
down the mountain....
The first two miles
were sheer ice,
straight down.

We came to the bottom. It was very rocky. . . .

After a while,
the blizzard stopped.

We walked and walked, until we came to the ocean.
We were wet and tired, so we decided to rest.

When I woke up, the egg had floated away. We swam after it.

Unfortunately, a sea monster had spotted it.

The sea monster was about to eat it when along came *another* sea monster.

I was able to rescue the egg.

We swam over to a big rock. It turned out to be...

a *third* sea monster! But it was nice, and it gave us a ride to shore...

through town, and . . .

right to our front door just as . . .

Charlotte was coming out to look for eggs."

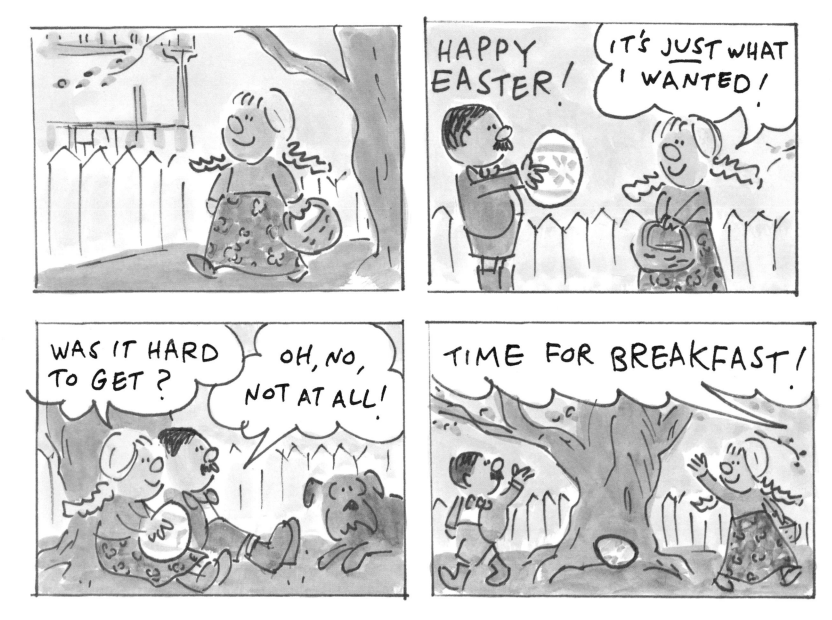